Queen Dög

words by **Bridget Heos** • illustrations by **Alejandro O'Keeffe**

Dᴉsney · HYPERION

Los Angeles   New York

First Edition, January 2017
10 9 8 7 6 5 4 3 2 1
FAC-029191-16258
Printed in Malaysia

Library of Congress Cataloging-in-Publication Data

Heos, Bridget.
  Queen Dog / by Bridget Heos ; illustrated by Alejandro O'Keeffe.
      pages cm
  Summary: Queen Dog must adjust to not being the center of attention when a new baby arrives.
  ISBN 978-1-4847-2852-9
  [1. Dogs—Fiction. 2. Babies—Fiction. 3. Kings, queens, rulers, etc.—Fiction.] I. O'Kif, illustrator. II. Title.
  PZ7.H4118Qu 2017
  [E]—dc23   2014046488

For Ben, a prince of a dog
—B.H.

To all the puppies of the world. Without them, life would be really very heavy.
And to my three Queen dogs: Hendy, Evelyn, and Sweety.
—A.O.

Once upon a time, there lived a beautiful princess.

With loving hands, she was raised to be noble and good.

Before long, she was crowned Queen Dog.

The brave and adventurous Queen Dog led her people on quests for great treasure.

She organized royal hunts.

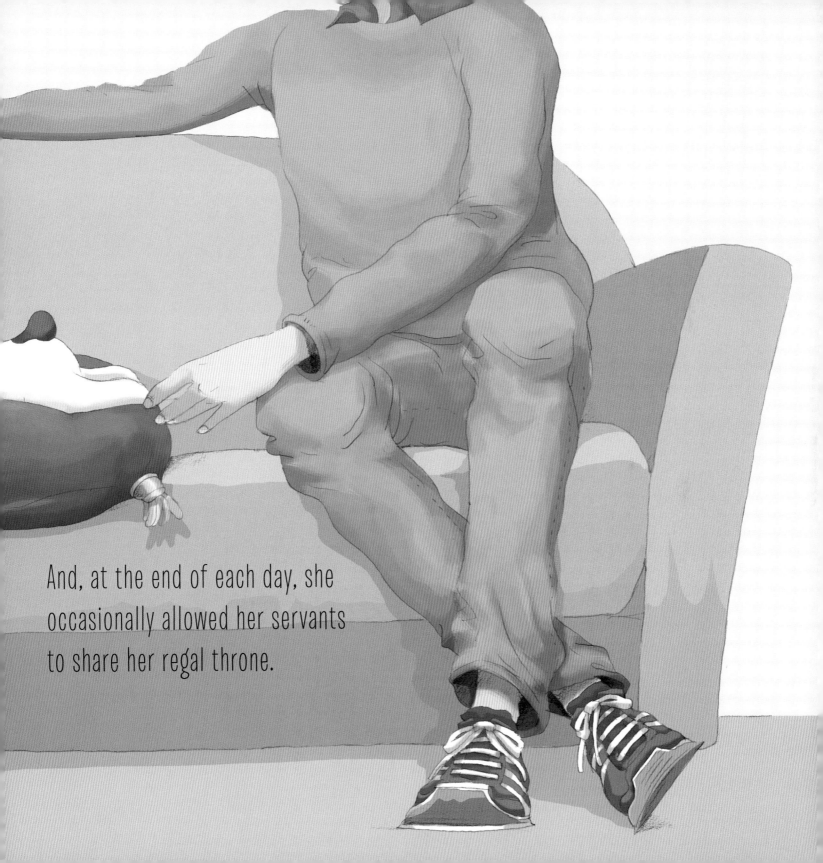

And, at the end of each day, she occasionally allowed her servants to share her regal throne.

Being queen had its perks.

Her servants brought her delicious meals on
silver platters,

washed her in the royal baths,

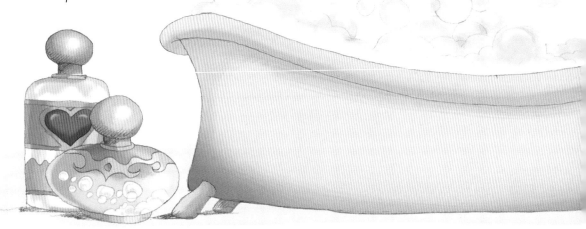

and presented her with
the most lavish gifts.

Life was fairy-tale perfect.

Well, almost.

Honestly, service had gone a bit downhill as of late.
Hunts had decreased from three to two a day.

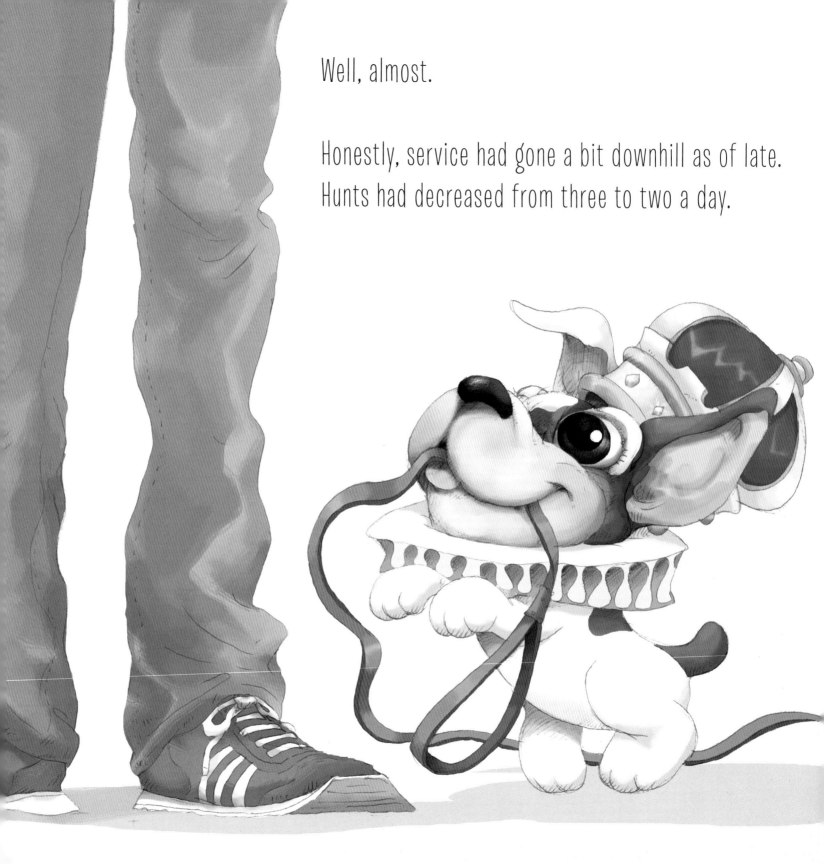

Once or twice, Queen Dog was forced
to prepare her own dinner.

And worst of all, her throne was always
covered in rags.

But then, grand news! A visitor arrived from afar. Her name was Catherine. The queen couldn't wait to sip tea with this proper young lady!

As it turned out, however, the guest wasn't proper at all.

She was extremely loud.

And when she finally quieted down, she was a complete snore!

Even worse, Queen Dog's servants were constantly distracted by this newcomer.

They were supposed to be preparing for a
royal ball, yet the castle was a mess!

Queen Dog thanked her lucky stars when new servants came to help.
Perhaps they would show the others how to serve a queen!

Indeed, they cleaned and cooked

and opened the castle doors
for the royal guests.

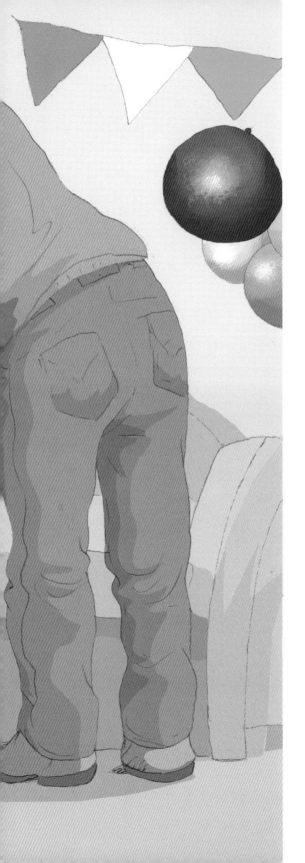

There was feasting and laughter, and
. . . presents for Queen Dog!

A shimmering wand? How regal!
But what was this? They were giving the
wand to that noisy girl!

Well!

Queen Dog had had it with this guest. It was time to ask her, very politely, to leave (and leave Queen Dog's wand behind).

But just then,

a thief stole the wand for himself!

This would not do.

Queen Dog seized the treasure from the scoundrel . . .

and gave it to Catherine, who smiled radiantly.

Queen Dog decided then that Catherine would be more than just an ordinary guest. She would live in the castle as the queen's princess-in-training.

From that day forward, Queen Dog escorted
Princess Catherine on all her journeys,

taught her good table manners,

and occasionally let her sit on the throne (for practice).

But most of all, Queen Dog was a loyal friend
to the princess,

as was fitting for a queen.